JACK'S TALE

ELLEN STOLL WALSH

HARCOURT BRACE & COMPANY

San Diego   New York   London

Requests for permission to make copies
of any part of the work should be mailed to:
Permissions Department, Harcourt Brace & Company,
6277 Sea Harbor Drive, Orlando, Florida 32887-6777.

Library of Congress Cataloging-in-Publication Data
Walsh, Ellen Stoll.
Jack's tale/Ellen Stoll Walsh.
p. cm.
Summary: An author begins to write a fairy tale and
finds that the main character, Jack, must be convinced
to participate in the story and help rescue the princess.
ISBN 0-15-200323-1
[1. Fairy tales. 2. Characters in literature—Fiction.]
I. Title.
PZ8.W1785Jac 1997
[E]—dc20   95-43255

First edition   A B C D E F

Printed in Singapore

The illustrations in this book are
cut-paper collage.
The display type was set in Herculanum.
The text type was set in Garamond Light.
Color separations by United Graphic, Singapore
Printed and bound by Tien Wah Press, Singapore
This book was printed on totally
chlorine-free Nymolla Matte Art paper.
Production supervision by Stanley Redfern
Designed by Camilla Filancia

For
PAUL J. JONES,
my stepfather, and granddad
to all our kids

Once, not long ago, an author sat down to write
a fairy tale. Ideas bounced around like rubber balls.
A princess bounced. Trolls bounced. And Jack bounced.

"Wait a minute!" said Jack. "Leave me out. Fairy tales aren't safe—I saw those trolls."

"I *need* trolls," said the author. "Now be still, and don't complain. You're the main character. You'll be famous."

Famous sounded good to Jack. "Okay, write your story," he said. "Just promise not to scare me."

"Sorry. I don't make promises," said the author. "Anything can happen in a fairy tale."

"Well, write fast then, so we can get this over with."

The author smiled. "Now listen, Jack. Here's all you have to do. Go through the story one page at a time. Start at the beginning, go through the middle, and stop when you reach the end. And, Jack…be extra careful in the middle."

With that advice, the author picked up her pencil. "Once upon a time...," she began.

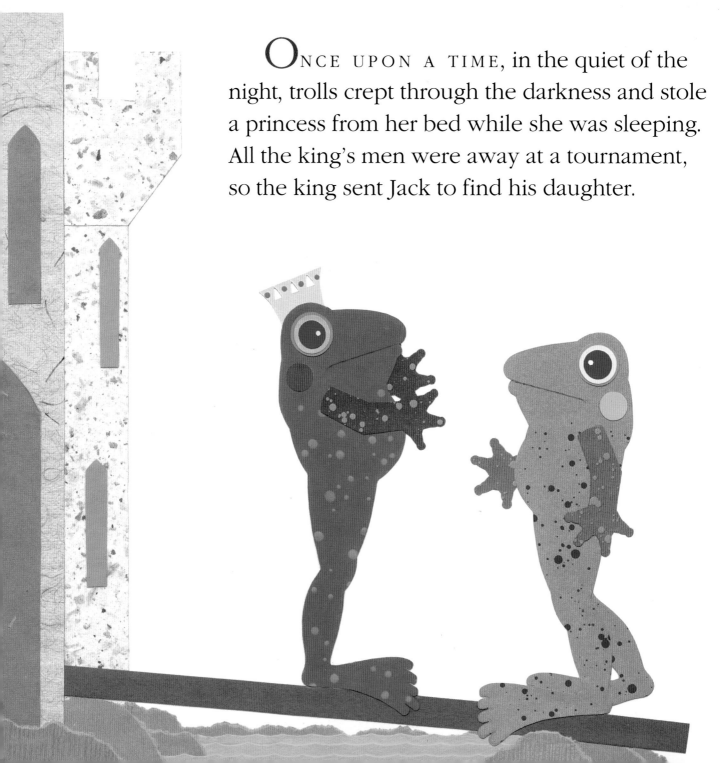

ONCE UPON A TIME, in the quiet of the night, trolls crept through the darkness and stole a princess from her bed while she was sleeping. All the king's men were away at a tournament, so the king sent Jack to find his daughter.

"So far, so good," Jack said to himself. "It's a wonderful day to rescue a princess. I'm right behind you, trolls." And off he marched.

He kept on until he met an old frog.
"Go back," the old frog warned. "Back to where you
came from. There are trolls up ahead, and
they've got the princess."

"I can't go back. I am on my way to *rescue* the princess. The king himself has sent me. If I go back, my story will end at the beginning."

"Well," said the old frog. "Do as you please. But don't get caught. Once you have been somebody's dinner, you'll be absolutely useless."

Jack shivered. But it was still a beautiful day to
rescue a princess, and he was soon back in high spirits.

As he walked, green hills and meadows gave way to rocks and dirt.

By nightfall Jack had reached the middle of the book.
The trolls were already there.
Jack settled down against a rock and slept. Poor Jack,
with danger all around him.

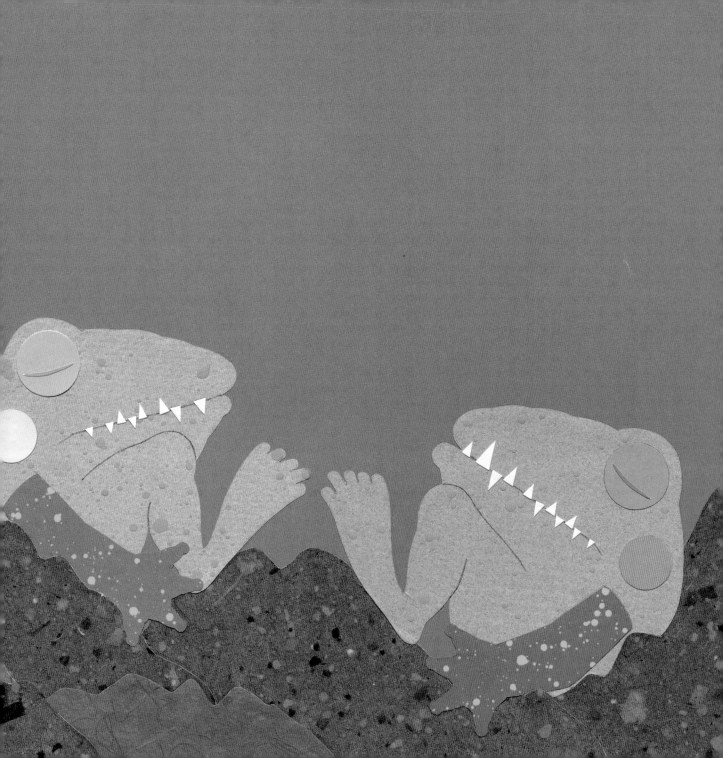

Jack woke up.
So did the danger.

The trolls got so close to Jack that his skin prickled. But they didn't catch him. The trolls were fast, but Jack was faster.

"It isn't easy to rescue a lost princess," Jack sighed.

But when he heard a sob, a sweet, sad sound, he followed it…

…until he found the princess. The trolls kept watch. And they were arguing.

"Why didn't you catch the other one?" snarled the big troll. "The one called Jack."

"Me? Why is it always me?" whined the other.

"Because it always *is* you," snapped the first. "Now we have only the princess. She's not enough to make a good frog pie."

The trolls were so busy yelling and screaming and pinching and slapping, they didn't see Jack untie the princess.

Jack and the princess ran and ran until they were close to the end of the story.

They made it safely. It wasn't far. The king proclaimed Jack a hero, and the princess gave him her hand in marriage. The book was finished.

Because everything worked out so well, Jack forgave the author.

And they all lived happily ever after.